This book is for

_____

From

_____

My wish for you is

_____

_____

To Isa—I wish you to always be your full self.

Copyright © 2020 by Andrea Pippins
All rights reserved. Published in the United States by Schwartz & Wade Books,
an imprint of Random House Children's Books, a division of Penguin Random House LLC, New York.
Schwartz & Wade Books and the colophon are trademarks of Penguin Random House LLC.

Visit us on the Web! rhcbooks.com
Educators and librarians, for a variety of teaching tools, visit us at RHTeachersLibrarians.com

*Library of Congress Cataloging-in-Publication Data*
Name: Pippins, Andrea, author. Title: Who will you be? / Andrea Pippins.
Description: First edition. | New York: Schwartz & Wade Books, [2020] |
Audience: Ages 3–6. | Summary: "A picture book about how family and community help shape
the wonderful people our children become"— Provided by publisher.
Identifiers: LCCN 2019033627 | ISBN 978-1-9848-4948-9 (hardcover) |
ISBN 978-1-9848-4949-6 (library binding) | ISBN 978-1-9848-4950-2 (ebook)
Subjects: CYAC: Individuality—Fiction. | Family life—Fiction. | Community life—Fiction. | Parent and child—Fiction.
Classification: LCC PZ7.1.P569 Who 2020 | DDC [E]—dc23

The text of this book is set in 25-point Adobe Garamond Premier.
The illustrations were rendered in pen and then modified and colored digitally.
Book design by Rachael Cole

MANUFACTURED IN CHINA
2 4 6 8 10 9 7 5 3
First Edition

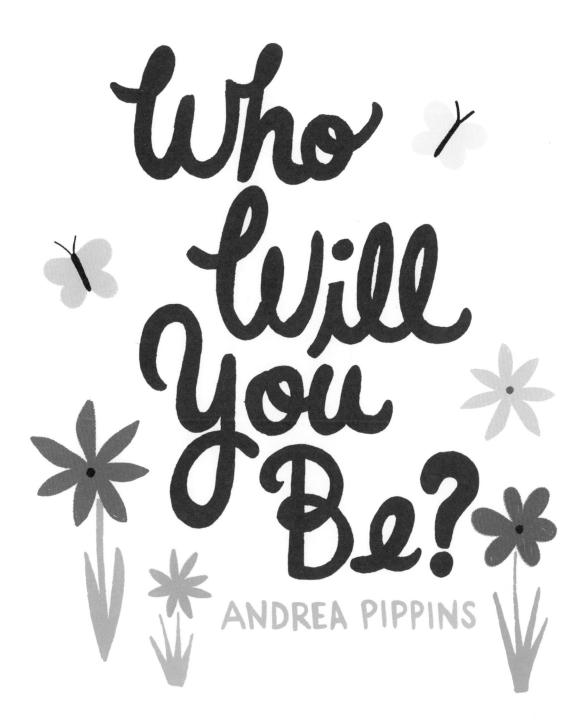

# Who Will You Be?

## ANDREA PIPPINS

schwartz & wade books · new york

My child, my little one,
who will you be when you are grown?

There's loving kindness
in your eyes, like your daddy's.

And boldness in your heart,
like your grandma.
Will you be like them?

Your cousin Curlena is loud and joyful.
Will you be like her?

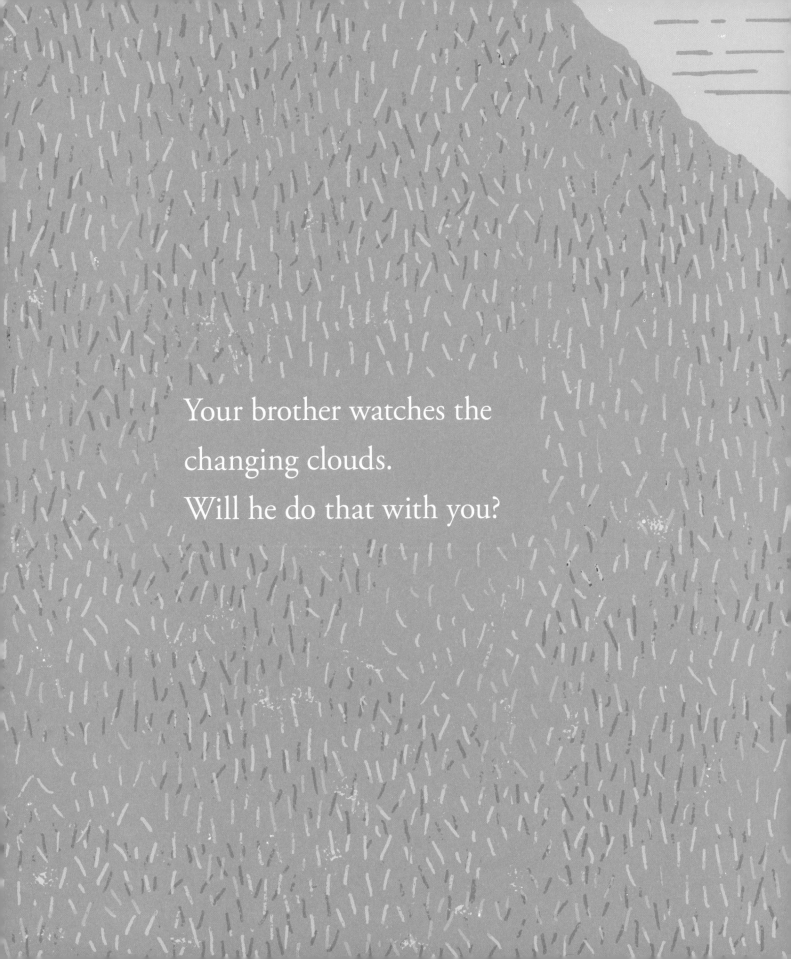

Your brother watches the
changing clouds.
Will he do that with you?

When you blow me a kiss,
you are loving, like your grandpa . . .

and your cousin Gigi,
who gives big hugs.

Your big dark eyes take in the world.
Will you be curious, like your uncle . . .

find beauty in all that you see,

like Ms. Jess . . .

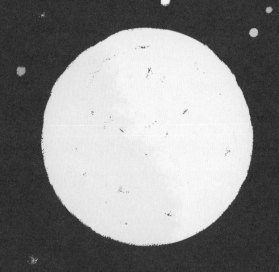

and be bound for
adventure, like your auntie?

Amina makes cakes and pies—will you do that, too?

Will you be compassionate,
like Alessandra?

And, Little One, will you be grateful,
oh so grateful, like me?

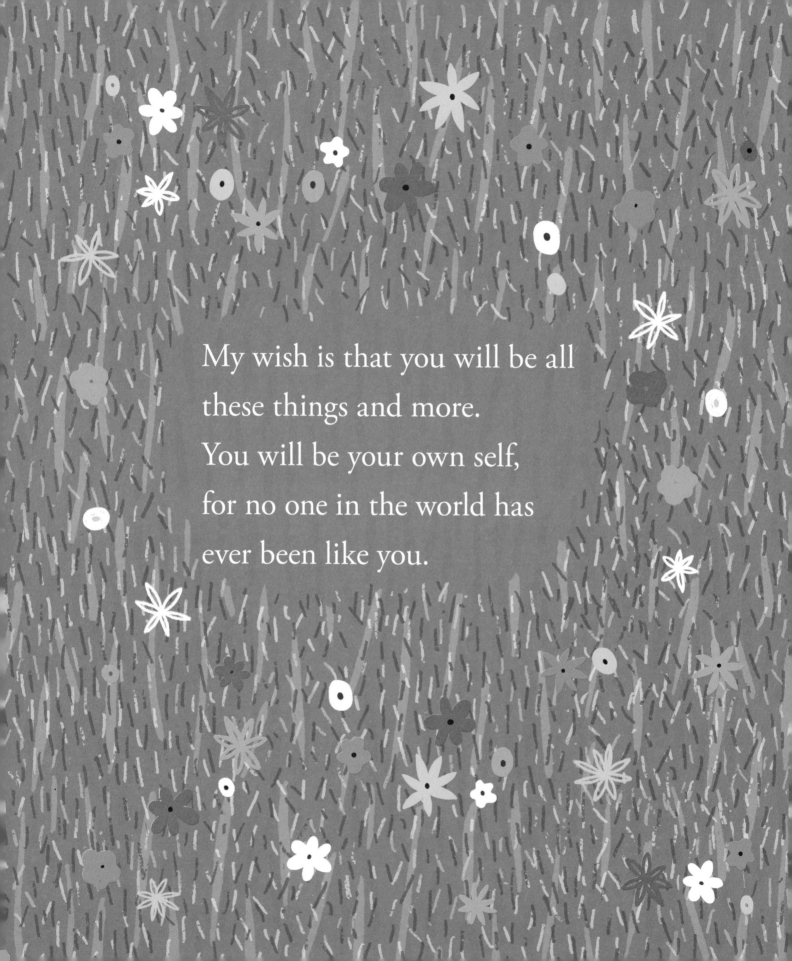

My wish is that you will be all
these things and more.
You will be your own self,
for no one in the world has
ever been like you.

And this I know, my child:
whoever you will be,
I will love you forever.